AF072989

:1473:

Written by Bedia Ceylan Güzelce

Translated by Mark David Wyers

Kingston University Press,
Kingston University
Penrhyn Road, Kingston upon Thames
Surrey KT1 2EE

© Bedia Ceylan Güzelce 2016

The right of the above author to identified as the author of this work has been asserted in accordance with the Copyright, Design and Patent Act 1988.

British Library Cataloguing in Publication Data available.

ISBN 978-975-6006-78-8

Cover designed by © Alosia Mazzolini

All rights reserved. No part of this publication may be produced, stored in or introduced into a retrieval system, or transmitted, in any form, or by any means electronic, mechanical, photocopying, recording or otherwise, without the prior permission of the publisher. Any person who commits any unauthorised act in relation to this publication may be liable to criminal prosecution and civil claims for damages.

To my father, Yaşar Mehmet Güzelce

Dear reader,
    like the hedgehogs
        who kicked up dust
            as they trod the land
        in Otlukbeli,
    we were never mentioned
in the history.

1473

HASAN BEG OF THE AKKOYUNLU DYNASTY

In the sixth month of the year 1423, in the lands ruled by the Akkoyunlu Empire, a child who would be named Hasan tore himself from his mother's womb, impatient to behold the wonders of the world. Angels swooped down and surrounded him, drawing out his limbs with all their might. He thus became one of the tallest men of the fifteenth century, even though he'd been born to a family as squat as wine barrels.

God commanded and the angels complied. Like his grandfather, Kara Yölük Osman Beg, Hasan was destined to breathe life and wealth into the Akkoyunlu dynasty. As a child he would grow feverish when upset, and his eyebrows would arch like the wings of a crane. Hasan was of such beauty that people who saw him just once would long to die and be reborn so they could see him again in the next life. Until that summer of 1423, such a radiant child had never graced the lands of the Akkoyunlu, which extended from Akşehir to Erzurum and from Bayburt to Nusaybin. Women would get pregnant again and again in the hopes that their children would look like him, or they would give up on having children altogether, fearing that none could ever be his peer.

Weary of the arguments his father perpetuated with his brothers, Hasan proclaimed that one day he would rule Diyarbakır, the capital of the empire, as

1473

well as all the Akkoyunlu people. When he did become the leader, one of his greatest achievements was to defeat Jahan Shah, the ruler of the Karakoyunlu. He then moved the capital to Tabriz. He was the living incarnation of the greatness of Genghis and Tamerlane. And like all great conquerors, his triumphs were heralded in verse. It was said that he had been selected by God, and many believed he was the chosen one. But as the borders of his empire expanded, so did the animosity of the Ottomans. Under his command, the Turkmens of Eastern Anatolia moved to Iran and Central Asia, where they would live for hundreds of years.

Hasan read the work of all the poets of the east and knew their poems by heart. With his subjects he was honest of speech and openly spoke his mind, and he always kept the calmest of demeanour. He shared all he knew, making no distinction between young and old, uneducated and scholarly. When he fell silent, it was like the silence before the toppling of a thousand trees. Hasan put an end to thievery and gambling, crimes that had run rampant under the rule of the Karakoyunlu. He was also beloved by his people because he protected mosques from the attacks that had before been commonplace.

In the past, trade routes had been harried by bandits but he flushed them out and caravans could now travel in safety. Whenever his subjects heard that Hasan was journeying through their lands they would set out days in advance just to get a chance to see him, even if from a distance. And those lucky

1473

few who got close enough bore witness to a thin trail of smoke scented of cedar and linden that rose up from his very being, as he had been so blessed at birth. This smoke rose up like an arrow and smote the hearts of all his adoring subjects, making the eternal blood of love flow.

He first married Despina Khatun, the beautiful niece of David who was the last emperor of Pontic Greek Trebizond, for political reasons and after that he was wedded with Selçuk Begüm Sultan for love. Like some creatures of the Earth who are ever faithful, until his death he loved only her. Seven sons were born to them: Ughurlu Muhammad, Maqsud Beg, Yaqub Beg, Masih Beg, Mirza Khalil, Yusuf Beg, and Zeynel Beg.

Hasan rebuilt every city he conquered and spoke with the artisans, discussing matters of state with them before anyone else. Divination was of great import for him, and he summoned soothsayers from the four corners of the empire to the capital. He enacted laws so fair that they were maintained in the lands he ruled well after his death, and they inspired the ordering of many new states to come.

He believed that no man should go through life without enjoying the boon of a woman's bosom, so he encouraged the young to marry and large weddings were held in the spring under his command.

In 1473, he assembled his troops in Otlukbeli for the largest battle of his rule. He drew upon all the experience he had accrued in his fifty-year life. Two thoughts weighed heavy upon his mind: Ensuring

1473

that no harm came to his sons and that the blissful life of the Akkoyunlu people would spread through Anatolia. During those days of tumult, the people had faith in their leader.

When Hasan succumbed to an illness during a campaign in 1478, he died shortly after in Tabriz. If anyone had asked him, he would have said, "I died of love". Still, not once did he take his grandson Ismail into his arms, the son of his daughter Catherina Halima. But Ismail, who would one day become Shah, did appear to Hasan in his dreams.

1473

MEHMED THE CONQUEROR

As Mehmed the Conqueror entered the castle of the Byzantines, his heart was pounding and the soles of his feet were damp with sweat. The siege had dragged on for weeks. His genius had been proven when he ordered his men to carry their ships overland, thus bypassing the chains that the Byzantines had surreptitiously stretched across the Golden Horn. Such a tactic could have only been the work of a madman or Mehmed the Conqueror. Constantinople, the capital of the Byzantines, was of utmost importance for the Islamic world. Legend said that whoever conquered the city would bring peace to the soul of the Kaaba. This great duty had fallen upon the shoulders of Mehmed, who thereby attained the highest rank in the Islamic world as the blessed soldier of God. As he realized this dream, long been cherished by the Ottomans, Mehmed, the beloved son of Sultan Murad II and Hüma Valide Hatun, was filled with pride and ecstasy. His soldiers bellowed, "Rome! Rome!" They were eager for ever more victories. But while courage beat through his heart, a weariness bore down upon him. It was a weariness that could not easily be overcome. He simply did not have the strength to press on to Rome.

During the battle he had been struck in the chest, and the blood oozing from the wound gathered in his navel. It was as if his stomach, not his heart, was bleeding. Like all the Ottoman soldiers, his hands and his face were scratched and scored,

1473

and his entire body was covered in scars. Such scars were the hallmark of a man's dignity. That is how it was.

When he spoke, his voice would forever echo in your ears, never to be forgotten, like the most beautiful of birdsongs. He spoke little but was often deep in thought, and he was fond of music and poetry. When he listened to a lovelorn poet recite a passionate poem, his thoughts would wander far afield. Ah Mehmed Beg, it was clear that your thoughts were troubled.

As he passed through the courtyards of the palace, women and boys could not turn their eyes from him, and yet they longed to hide their faces from his regal gaze. In the presence of his fury, stones would tremble and plants would cease their whispering chatter. As he strode across the face of the Earth, it was as if all eyes obediently watched this mighty sovereign.

Mehmed enjoyed feeling the lands he conquered beneath his feet and indulged himself in that pleasure. He delighted in splendour, rare cloth, precious stones, and architecture of a monumental scale. He built worthy places of worship and always yearned for minarets to tower into the sky. He spent long hours inside such mosques but never ascended their heights. Never. He was afraid of heights—that was his one and only fear.

As he walked, flowers would cast ever more lovely scents into the air so that he could breathe them in, the wind would sweep the way before him so that he would not stumble, clouds would hide

1473

behind the sun, and time would slow to a trickle. The sun shining on his face filled him with joy, for he believed that light was always auspicious. Only two people had seen his large, languorous eyes up close. One was his mother and the other was his lover, Sitti Hatun. Whenever he plucked a rose for Sitti, he deliberately cut his finger on one of the thorns and then pressed his bloodied finger onto the leaves of the stem, as if to say that only love could penetrate the armour of the skin.

Twenty years after conquering Constantinople, he began preparing for what may have been the largest battle of his reign. While he was now in his forties and had grown heavy and more weary over the years, anyone who saw him still could not help but gaze upon him admiringly. He had no choice but to confront Hasan, who had established a strong empire in Eastern Anatolia. As the Akkoyunlu people expanded, they were now posing a threat to the Ottomans. If need be, he was ready to sacrifice his life for his kin and fellow believers.

In 1481, traitors poisoned this majestic figure. At least, that is what some people whispered. But of course, what really killed the Conqueror was love. As the chief physician was trying to make the exhausted sultan as comfortable as possible in his last hours , a wound appeared on the sultan's chest; it was as large as the face of his lover. Baffled, the physician did not know how to treat this wound, the likes of which he had never seen before.

1473

OTLUKBELI
THE PLAIN

Wounds throb with the beating of our hearts. As for the world's heart, it beats on battlefields. In 1473, Otlukbeli became the heart of the world for eight hours. It pounded, pounded, and then stopped. Dead.

For months it had been clear that war was imminent. Hasan had grown strong in the east and was encroaching on Ottoman lands. Every move he made suggested that he wanted to be the sultan of Anatolia and the whole Islamic world, just as Mehmed the Conqueror did. For both of them, war was inevitable and justified.

Otlukbeli was ill suited for what would be one of the bloodiest clashes in history. Nearly two hundred thousand soldiers crowded into that narrow plain. More than one hundred thousand of these were ready to sacrifice themselves for the Ottoman Empire, while nearly seventy thousand of them had gone there to die for the Akkoyunlu Empire. The moustaches of every man on the battlefield concealed sweat borne of a fear of death. None of these thousands of men seeing each other for the first time truly understood why they were fighting.

Turks fought Turks and Muslims battled Muslims; some interpreted this as a sign that Judgement Day was looming near. Among those heroic soldiers, there were thousands of animals that had been unable to flee, and among those animals

1473

there were two hedgehogs. Of those hedgehogs, which had grown up thinking that they would either die dreaming or falling in love, there was one particular female and male. But as with all living creatures, their love knew nothing of gender. When the soldiers clashed on the plain, these two hedgehogs were also pulled into the battle, just like the other animals of Otlukbeli, and the battle raged above their burrow. Like the victory-crazed soldiers who lined up to kill each other, they prayed as they fell to the ground to be reborn in a world of immortality. And after every prayer, the animals said "so be it" instead of "amen."

So be it.

1473

History is an old man who
 does not remember anyone,
and only those who write history
 actually believe in him.

1473

My lover is mine, and I am my lover's. We drink from underground springs, and sometimes we feed on worms and at other times on roots. We spend our lives amidst a scent that is damp and deep. When you breathe in this scent, you discern the dead, the healing springs that will gush forth in a few days, and the groans of flowers that need just one more tincture of water to bloom. Working together, animals carry water down their tunnels to every root so that they can blossom. One by one. Each animal is responsible for its own plant, for making sure that it flowers. If need be, my lover would dig for days but he always watered our plant so that not a single leaf would wither. When my lover did this, I fell in love with him all over again, falling in love with his virility and his tender care for our burrow.

Without exception, we hedgehogs are devoted to a single lover. I know that my lover loves no one but me. That knowledge makes me stronger than other animals, even stronger than lions. My lover is my world; I long to give him hoglets and with that love protect our burrow from snakes, centipedes and other such creatures that roam the world. But I do not hold anything against them. Such creatures suffer from boundless solitude and drive everything before them whether dead or alive, and if they come across something they want, they devour it, seeing it as their birthright. I accept all that is a right of birth.

We have no hoglets yet, and judging by the stomping up above, it is not the time. Rumours of war are spreading. All of the animals living both

1473

below and above ground have been speaking of it for days now. The other morning I heard two foxes gossiping. I had hidden deep among some bushes and they did not catch my scent. They were saying that thousands, even tens of thousands of soldiers were preparing to go to war right above our burrows. You could not point out a single animal living on these lands that does not know the meaning of war. We spent our childhoods listening to stories about battles. Yes, I said "childhood". We animals also have childhoods.

It all began three winters ago. As always, I went to sleep at the end of autumn, slipping into hibernation as I have always done since I was born, but at the end of that particular winter I awoke as a woman longing for love. I escaped outside to breathe in fresh air and shake off the grogginess of months of sleeping. It was dusk. Hedgehogs usually doze during the day and go out as the sun sets. That evening I was wandering through thick undergrowth on the shores of Otlukbeli Lake. I stopped, raising my head up as far as my neck would allow, and gazed up at the trees. Cedars towered ever upward and a sharp scent drifted through the air among their trunks. The reflections of poplars stretched out over the lake, resting on the still surface.

The green leaves budding from the branches of the trees could be seen in reflections on the water. You could see every detail: the veins through which life passes, and the bright green shrouds surrounding the veins. The trees of Otlukbeli grew up jostling each other ever so slightly, leaning out over the lake. If it weren't for those reflections, we hedgehogs would never know what the tops of trees look like. They were inaccessible to us, beyond our line of sight.

That was the perfect evening to fall prey to the wiles of love.

We always knew which animals had passed by not just by their scent but by their tracks as well. Wild pigs left deep gouges in the mud. By lowering my ear to the ground I could hear the clamour of their hooves. They were the most terrifying of all the animals of Otlukbeli and we knew the very least about them. The wild pigs would emerge at night and with frightening grunts and snorts they would ravage the forest. The first order of business before the break of dawn would be to repair the burrows that had been damaged in the night. Work had to start, especially for animals whose burrows easily collapsed, such as ants and mice. Everything else in the world grew older, but Otlukbeli was built anew every day. Ceremonial prayers for those who lost their lives in the night would then commence. And after every prayer, the animals said "so be it" instead of "amen."

So be it.

It had two meanings. "So be it" meant that we accepted everything as it is and "so be it" how passionately we wanted our prayers to come true.

1473

And I devoted
    myself to
        him.

1473

The evening sun hummed a song the sound of a deep "e", and I drew closer to the water's edge. Without hesitating I plunged my head deep into the vast coolness before me. Those waters were one of the secret depositories of the Euphrates River, the headwaters of which were not far away. But it provided no escape for the water and went on existing as a lake. Otlukbeli Lake. This is where we caught our first and only glimpses of frogs, freshwater creatures and trout. The pace of life underwater was frantic and beyond my comprehension. Those animals were always in such a rush. With flicks of their tails they flitted about like birds, soaring through the water.

As on every evening, Otlukbeli Lake was illuminated by fireflies and the light reflected from the backs of lizards revealed their silhouettes. The water washed away my weariness as I held my breath and my body was brought back to life. When God first breathed life into me, my body swelled, and yet I was shorter than poppies in bloom and longer than the stones scorpions hide under. That's how it is for all hedgehogs, and that's why our slender feet carry our divinity within.

When I grew weary of observing the extraordinary underwater scene before me and started to run out of breath, I raised my head from the water. I reopened my eyes to the world and at that moment I heard a deep, young voice, the voice of my lover-to-be, as he greeted me.

I gazed at his unrivalled beauty, his divine bodily form. Each and every one of his quills was

1473

radiant like a minaret rising into the sky. Sometimes these minarets topple down and lay flat, and at other times they stand straight up. If you look from far enough away, minarets rising up from a dome are similar in appearance to our quills. The male hedgehog in front of me was much larger than me, magnificent and powerful. Time seemed to be standing still. At once I chose him, and he chose me. When your heart becomes overwhelmed by love, you need to feel it with all five senses to be convinced that it's actually real. You catch a scent, you hear a sound and you taste something both sweet and sour on your tongue. You take pride in your eyes beholding such beauty and you feel the ground slipping away beneath you, like silk.

My lover gazed at me with the whole world in his eyes. Those eyes had been created in an underground city of a thousand passageways and could do no evil. Even if I were presented with all the radiant beings of the world I would immediately be able to tell you which eyes were his. With a single glance he could transform a cluster of herbs into an elixir, and he could turn a handful of worthless stones into a treasure. He could do it all so easily that as it happened before your very eyes, you wouldn't hear a single sound. My lover always had a word at the ready. And that day, he said:

"Good morning."

My lover and I spent the entire evening quill-to-quill on the plain. As his quills brushed up against mine, not once jabbing into my flesh, I knew that

he also had fallen in love with me. From the first time he had managed to find the proper distance. Sometimes it can take two hedgehogs weeks to get it right and not hurt each other. As my heart was filled with his being, there was no room left for anything else. I forgot my mother, my father, and my siblings. I forgot the companions I had bedded down with for the winter hibernation. As they slipped from my heart, my lover filled it up. Next it was time for God. O forgive me, Lord. It was time to bid farewell to the God who had given me my quills, the God who had protected and looked after my soul. By the end of that night, as I became bound to my lover, I was embalmed in my love. And I called out:
    - God,
        if you lean down a little,
                I will embrace you.

1473

O Lord,
        when you breathed
                life into us,
      surely you had a plan
in mind.

1473

We, two hedgehogs, had drifted off to sleep. And God leaned down. Exactly one day had passed since I met my lover. When God leaned down, a giant mirror appeared before me and I saw that his chest and Otlukbeli were one and the same. When we awoke, my lover and me belonged to one another. The joining of yet another male and female had taken place in the world. That's just how simple it was, without celebration, wedding, or ritual. The buzzing of flies in the sky was the same. The snails still struggled to move through the mud, and as always, the earth soaked up the purple silky trails they left behind. Worms were born purple with that liquid. Nature intermingled with itself because it had no one else.

My lover is mine, and I am my lover's. Otlukbeli is the breast of God, and we stretched out on His plain. Back then, the importance of plains fell away, the height of a mountain meant little, and I forgot how ancient the trees really were. All life for which you are responsible silently pulls away. On a night like that we made love, embraced, plunged, and arose, but never once forgetting our land, Otlukbeli. Ah Otlukbeli, you who pass through the heart of God. Falling in love on that night was akin to conceiving a child that would never be born. A child of eternity. My quills, my claws, my ears were pregnant. I craved soil. There was Otlukbeli, and there was my lover. I longed to devour the earth gliding beneath me and give birth with my entire body. I knew that if you love someone like your own land, you learn to make do with a handful of earth. I learned this.

All creatures in nature try to make themselves visible to the eyes of God. Birds build magnificent nests in the hope that God will notice them, and plants try to outdo each other in the colour of their foliage and the taste of their fruit. Eagles soar with hardly a flap of their wings so that God will admire them, worms tunnel through the earth, fish hurl themselves high into the air, peacocks screech... All so that their existence will be known. Disappearing from sight is only the work of creatures of the dark. These creatures are proud, powerful beings who have no fear of angering God. And on the day when they find themselves in need of God, they know that upon this proclamation, they will be rushed to his side:

"Second chances are taken, not given."

Once they learn this, God gives even those fearless ones another chance.

We hedgehogs dig burrows deep underground. The most robust hedgehog lives eighteen years at most, so our lives are precious. According to who? For example, according to turtles. We haven't seen it for ourselves but we hear that they live three hundred years. Meanwhile, we feed well, eating the tender roots of vegetables and drinking the pure water that trickles down through the seven layers of Earth. We emerge from our burrows at night when most of the other creatures are asleep, longing for God to see our quills gleaming in the moonlight like earthly stars. Far, far above is the sky and within it is God. As soon as we are born we know that. And we never let anyone get between us and God. We are devout but have no prophets.

Trees are the only way to ascend to the sky, God's abode. God often summons squirrels, leopards, and even ants to his side, and they scamper up the trees, sometimes not returning for days or weeks. Like every creature dedicated to God, we envy their privilege. And like every creature, we can understand a number of languages well but only speak our own. We can understand the languages of humans, cats, and birds. When ants return from their long journeys into the heavens, they speak of God—although it is true that they speak very little—and this keeps vibrant the image we have of him in our imaginations. God does not distinguish between the powerful and weak when he summons creatures to his side. For him, good and evil are far less important than we think.

We short-lived creatures see God and the beings that exist in his realm as greater than they actually are. He knows this. God is compassionate and while he does not deign to share his troubles with us he does love us. We hedgehogs, who among all of his creations were never granted the right to ascend to his level in heaven, believe that we have two hearts. And those hearts are so close together that not even a breath can pass between them. When we die and rise up into the sky, we give our second heart to a hedgehog we have shaped into being from water and air. Those tasteless, odourless elements are thus brought to life and heaven opens up. Hedgehogs condemned to hell, however, suffer in both of their hearts and feel twice as lonely and disconnected, suspended as they are in mid-air. All that is bad is twice as wicked for them. They have two eyes, and so twice they gaze upon distant horizons.

We hedgehogs are quite imaginative, and who knows, maybe that vivid imagination will be the death of us... I ascribed much meaning to the fact that my lover came into this world. I filled myself with him, to such an extent that there was no room left for anything else.

That's why I killed God that day. The sight of Him dead, tumbling towards the ground in a twisted tangle, never left my thoughts. Praying mantises caught hold of his frail frame at each end and held him up in the air, and he remained suspended there. I came eye to eye with His dead gaze. It was love that led me to kill Him. As you know, if there is love, no greater power can exist.

Whenever He is killed, praying mantises take His lifeless spirit and carry Him from place to place. When He is gone, the wind sets its enraged gaze on the realm of animals, planning which nests it will blow away and the hatchlings it will send tumbling to the ground. You can think of raging storms as divine rituals that are testaments to the wind's devotion to God. Birds speak of stormy worlds up there in the dark void above the sky, worlds called planets... It is said that the souls of winds, those that have blown their very last, take refuge on those planets where they lose themselves among holy spirits, drawing on their power to blow again and worship God. Just like all living creatures,winds never truly die. We hedgehogs understood very young that we have to protect ourselves against their fury. That's why the earliest hedgehog legends spoke of their terrifying power and wrath. We know that those storms, which are so violent that they can pluck up trees with roots reaching down to the centre of the earth, are actually sending word to God of every scent and sound. That's why, up until the time you kill him, God sees, hears, and understands everything.

1473

What else
        could hedgehogs
                prick their
        quills against
except love?

1473

Otlukbeli waited for three winters after my fate, and my lover's, was decided.

Roses waited,
healing herbs waited,
pregnant animals waited,
clouds waited,
even water waited...
Finches waited,
Martens, who were good at heart but of ill repute, waited,
men, women and children waited.
All, completely still.
Women waited, completely still.

Otlukbeli took a breath and held it with no intention of exhaling until the battle was over.

Before this befell us, we had seen small battles—that is, between animals. They tried to prove their strength to each other: bees and butterflies on fields of flowers, foxes and coyotes on the steppe, wolves and boars among boulders at night. I remember two hungry eagles who fought over a field mouse. But the impending disaster was to be like nothing else that had come before.

Each battle has its own particular language, its own letters, syllables, words, and sentences. A battle plays out in its own language and then comes to an end. Enemies exchange blows in this language and then die. They pray in this language, which no one else could ever know or understand, and the moment one side is victorious, they forget it. Only the underwater creatures can understand what

1473

is spoken in their realm, and it is the same on the battlefield; only those involved in the battle can ever know what really happened.

When fear overcame patience, both people and animals started to leave the plain. The turtles were the first to go. That year, some birds avoided Otlukbeli altogether.

Mice left,

moles left,

foxes, ants, and wild horses left.

Brightly coloured insects left, as did venomous snakes.

Children left, hoisted onto the backs of their fathers.

And hedgehogs left.

If animals unexpectedly migrate, you can be sure that a calamity is imminent. And that migration has a powerful scent. When it becomes strong enough it becomes a sound, sometimes it even becomes speech. When animals flee, they pray. But humans curse.

The only creatures that watched it all unfold from a distance, from the sky, were birds: griffon vultures, peregrines, bar-headed geese and bald eagles.

Hayyam was a griffon vulture almost as large as a human. His body was red and the inside of his wings had black bands, and with those colours he looked more like a volcano than a bird. When he wanted to fly he would first raise his wings and then, spinning in the opposite direction of the earth, take to the sky. He perched atop boulders dotted with lizards, whom God had granted the gift of being able to regrow their tails.

Like other griffon vultures, Hayyam fed on carrion. Because he could not, or would not, kill, he fed on the remains of creatures that had already been hunted down to satisfy his hunger. That we had never seen a dead griffon vulture made us think they were immortal. Since they were born with the ability to soar above the earth, birds would tell us land-bound creatures stories about what happened up in the sky. Such a messenger bird that came around like an emissary of nature could be anything from a turtledove to a magpie, or even a griffon vulture like Hayyam.

He came and went as he pleased, and whenever he flew overhead the animals of Otlukbeli would grow tense, sticking their heads out of their burrows and nests, breathing in panicked gasps. They thought that we were all about to die and Hayyam had come to eat us—but that was never going to happen. Hayyam brought us news about the outside world. Sometimes he warned us about an approaching storm, or mentioned that a flock of birds that feed on the wild animals of the steppe was drawing near, or told us spring would come early.

It was a day no different than all the others. Hayyam arrived in the morning. Even though he knew that we sleep during the day, he cawed loudly above our burrows, frightening most other animals away with his terrifying screech. We crawled outside and waited for him to land. Seen from below, he looked like a winged tree because he was so large. Like a soaring pine, he slowly descended towards us, flying in large lazy circles and then back through those circles again, perhaps saying a prayer of thanks for his ability to fly. Swirling like a dervish that is dutifully finishing his prayers, he landed nearby and began telling us about the Ottoman army approaching Otlukbeli:

"The Ottoman Sultan is wearing the grandest garments of silk, set with gemstones along the hem. Precious gems, semi-precious stones. His shoulders seem broad, but maybe that's just because of his attire. His gaze bears traces of the decisions he has made on his journey, and the worries that tug on his heart. Young soldiers, very young soldiers, surround him. I saw some in the rear ranks weeping. Some were weeping out of pride, others because of a heavy heart. Some were ill and others had eyes heavy with sleep. No one knows why they wept—no one could ever know. Clouds passed overhead and their tears fell to the grass. What was I saying? Ah yes! He is clearly the sultan. Sometimes he stops his horse and talks to his soldiers, speaking in long, drawn out sentences. Just like Uzun Hasan, he starts and ends every sentence by saying 'Allah.' He rarely blinks. Saddled on his horse, he appeared quite calm and majestic. He has brought many soldiers with him, and doctors too. And horses and herds of sheep. Sometimes he presses his hand to his heart as if he wants to take hold of it. Like Uzun Hasan, he is always gazing off into the distance..."

1473

If people could understand the language of birds, they would not go to war so often. My lover grew angry as Hayyam told us about the approaching army. I know he was worried for me, and everything that meant: our future children, our sons and daughters, and the songs we would sing together, as well as our days of health and illness. For the tales we would tell, the stories of heroism, and for our winter hibernation together. For waking up in the spring, and watching our children awake from their first hibernation. For their quills, every single one of them.

Hayyam told us that we should leave Otlukbeli. And right then my lover decided that we would stay. We would take certain precautions and wait for this disaster to pass away over our heads. We would dig our burrow even deeper and prepare stores of water. By stocking up on roots, we would be sure not to starve. Whatever happened in the world above, we were going to stay in Otlukbeli to spite those who thought that soldiers were the only ones who dared to brave the battlefield.

Seeing my lover so decisive made me proud but concern gripped my heart. As I looked at his face, I wanted nothing but to help him. Worry drove us to get ready, as if we ourselves were going to battle. While no one ever mentions us in the histories, we two hedgehogs prepared for battle in Otlukbeli, along with Uzun Hasan and Mehmed the Conqueror.

With those words, Hayyam flew up into the sky. We gazed admiringly at the green plumage of his

1473

chest and his wings. He could fly—what else could you want? At any moment he could fly up and away, so high that we became mere specks on the ground. That is why he was unruffled by the commotion and concern, and why no one in the world has ever seen birds going to battle. Nor their tears or rejoicing...

1473

Otlukbeli
     disappears,
          and then
               suddenly it
                    appears again.

1473

As they point to the sky, the hills tell us something. It is not in vain that at times the clouds mingle among us. If a mountain falls in love with a star, it fills with a smouldering fire that reduces everything around it to ashes—then it sputters outs and dies. The spirits of dead mountains are brought together with stars in Otlukbeli.

How many times can a mountain die? How many times can the same mountain fall in love with the same star? Where else could a love like that love in which I became one and the same as my lover happen but in Otlukbeli? That's why we stayed. And those mountains are the gravestones of seas. It is no easy task to ravage a plain; as for drying up a lake, that simply cannot be done. In the same way, the idea that a battle could take place in Otlukbeli seemed impossible to us.

Since spring, Hayyam had come to see us every day. We found out from Hayyam that Mehmed the Conqueror and Grand Vizier Mahmud Pasha had sent a large expeditionary force out to prepare for an incursion into the lands of the Akkoyunlu. Before setting off in the month of April on his eastern campaign across the Bosphorus, he had picked the top Janissaries to join the ranks of his army. Along the way, Has Murad Pasha and Davud Pasha joined his forces, as well as Prince Mustafa and Prince Bayezid. Their forces met up in Sivas, creating the largest Ottoman army ever to have been assembled.

Meanwhile, voluntary legions from chiefdoms around Anatolia swelled its ranks. The Ottomans set

1473

up camp in Erzincan, where they met with some slight resistance, but Uzun Hasan had ordered the people to surrender at first. They were to allow Mehmed the Conqueror to set up camp and then await a command from Uzun Hasan. As a result, the Ottoman warriors easily took Erzincan. By this time, the Ottoman army had grown as others from Anatolia joined in and it was nearly 150,000 strong, almost twice the size of the Akkoyunlu forces.

The Ottoman army was so large that it did not march. Instead, it flowed like a river. Wearing light cotton tunics, the soldiers were like butterflies on migration. Seven days before the huge battle took place, the Ottoman expeditionary force had tried to cross the Euphrates so as to attack the Akkoyunlu encampment, thinking the Akkoyunlu had set up their main camp there. As they tried to cross the river, they were ambushed and the soldiers scattered. Some drowned, others were killed, and yet others were taken prisoner. Those who survived returned in shame to Mehmed the Conqueror's camp in Erzincan. One side of the river was weighed down by feelings of rage, defeat, and fear, while the other side rejoiced, buoyed up by courage and victory.

But not enough soldiers had fallen yet, not those of Mehmed the Conqueror nor those of Uzun Hasan. As Mehmed's forces went north along the Euphrates, the Akkoyunlu army followed along on the opposite side of the river. The two armies warily eyed each other as they made their way forward on each side of the river, longing to slaughter their foes.

1473

Within a few hours, the Ottoman forces disappeared from sight. Like an invisible spirit, they marched to a place called Başkent and stopped. The Akkoyunlu forces, which were growing larger by the hour, returned to their main encampment. However, despite the new recruits the Akkoyunlu army was still much smaller than the Ottoman forces. Hayyam could tell the difference between the two armies because the Akkoyunlu wore red helmets while the Ottomans' were gold, and based on that he surmised who would win the war. If it had not been for Hayyam's wings, which were like starry skies, we never would have known any of this. He told us all that was happening, moment by moment.

1473

Anguished souls
       rushed toward
              the heart of God.

1473

That morning, the flowers pulled in their petals. Battle was coming the next day to Otlukbeli. You did not need ears like a bat to hear the pounding hearts of the soldiers in the Akkoyunlu army, which was surrounding the Ottoman troops in Başkent like a crescent moon. The sound of their hearts thudded against the trunks of trees and fell to the ground, making the roots of the trees tremble.

When day broke, my lover emerged from our burrow. He said he was going to Mehmed the Conqueror's camp and that he would be back by nightfall. My lover spoke fine words, true words, and he always accomplished what he said. Upon his return he told me all that he had seen:

"Mehmed the Conqueror has as many soldiers as glimmers of light on a river under a full moon.

"There are horses.

"Massive iron cannons.

"Guns.

"Gunpowder.

"Soldiers wearing helmets of gold.

"The largest tent belongs to the Sultan, and there are smaller ones as well. The Sultan's tent is made of goat hair, and it smells of herbs and leather. It has neither a beginning nor an ending as it towers up. But Hayyam could see how tall it is. They are drinking water from earthenware cups, and have long daggers slung from their belts. I am certain they always keep one hand on their daggers. Their feet are small, and they themselves are small, but there are so many of them. They speak loudly, and they are eloquent. It is as if their faces were shrouded in shadow. Their faces are lost, the embodiment of darkness. In that gloom there are thousands, tens of thousands, of gleaming eyes. They are close to the plain and our burrow.

"Hayyam was right. The battle will take place in Otlukbeli. The Ottomans have come to take these lands, all of them. They have turned each other's shadows into beds but they sit there and sleep because there's no room to lie down. One sleeps, and the other beside him is awake, eyes open. They are eating birds. They killed the birds and then built fires, and after that they put the birds over the fires for a while, probably waiting for them to die through and through. First they tear off the legs and the wings, and then eat what is left. They are eating rabbits and sheep in the same way. Some of them are even eating the heads of the birds, and the eyes too. This is not hunger, it cannot be. As I was coming back, one of my quills caught on the chest of a soldier who was in a deep sleep, as if he had been given a small dose of snake venom. Not enough to kill him, but just enough send him into a stupor. He was dreaming and talking in his sleep. I could not understand but I think he was murmuring the names of people. He was sighing, and even though it was not cold, he was trembling. So young, almost a child. I left the quill there because I knew that if I pulled it out he would wake up. It is obvious that he will die. His eyes are already closed to the deepest of sleeps."

1473

As my lover told me all this, for the first time I saw that he was afraid. His expression tense, he moved towards me, and then snuggled up even closer. Then he began breathing in my scent. I could tell that we were heading towards an end. Starting with my back, one by one he breathed in the scent of my quills from the base to the tip, taking long deep breaths. Some of them pricked his face, but I knew he did it on purpose. He always did that when he was upset.

Up close, he was taking in my very being. Lovingly, passionately, he was taking in all of my existence. It made me think of Noah and the flood, the drawn out deaths of trees, lamps lit at night that later snuff themselves out, invisible rivers the headwaters of which are known but come to a silent end. Where do all those rivers go? I thought of the story of how humans were banished from heaven because of love, how they fell to earth naked and utterly alone, and how we animals are always naked. The mere fact that he was breathing in my scent made me think that way. His pounding heart thudded against the ground. From now on, people would not speak of night and day but rather the dead and those who survived.

The tunnels and underground passages that we dug until morning led straight up to the battlefield. When day broke, my lover and I fell asleep, cuddled up at the head of the one of the passages we had dug.

1473

We did not move.
    My lover was
           bidding me farewell.

1473

OTLUKBELI
ABOVE THE TUNNELS

At night both armies ate bread dripping with oil. When they awoke in the morning, they drank water, prayed together, and recited the Kalimah Shahadat.

The crescent-shaped formation of the Akkoyunlu army had been used to defeat Jahan Shah, leader of the Karakoyunlu. First the right arm of the crescent would attack, followed by the left. The soldiers in the middle would strike the final deadly blow. But this time they were facing Mehmed the Conqueror, a man whose heart harboured no fear and whose mind was a rampart of belief in victory. Grand Vizier Mahmud Pasha had long known that the Akkoyunlu had surrounded the hill and that they were running dangerously low on provisions, and he made sure the Ottoman army was ready to strike. When he gave the order to fire, the bloodiest eight hours of these lands would begin.

At the very front were the Azap, a contingent of foot soldiers. They are easily recognizable by the conical hats they wear. Before cannons and guns were introduced into battle, they were the most important unit in the army. A male was conscripted from every neighbourhood of thirty homes and sent to war. That is how they got their name: Azap actually means "torture." So when the time came, these men were "summoned to torture." A declaration was made in the four corners of the empire and the

1473

conscripted men were told how they would serve in the army. Men selected to be Azap had to be single, of strong build, and honest. The neighbourhood that had chosen him to be sent to the army paid for the expenses he accrued while serving but they were exempt from taxes until the war came to an end. The Azap were skilled archers, and their arrows struck the first blow against the enemy. And as before, they were now in the front ranks in Otlukbeli.

Upon Mahmud Pasha's order the Azap started to climb the hill occupied by the enemy. Behind them came the cannon and gun brigades, the cavalry, and the main infantry. The Akkoyunlu on the right side of the crescent swept down the hill as their enemy approached. The Azap struck first, taking aim and letting loose a hail of deadly arrows that ascended so high that it was not just arrows that rained down on the Akkoyunlu soldiers, but dead birds as well. Shields were useless. The arrows pierced feet, hands, and throats, some plunging into hearts and emerging from the soldiers' backs. Then the cannons boomed and the infantry began their ascent.

Every cannonball that blasted craters in Otlukbeli Plain took out tens of soldiers and knocked down trees that were a thousand years old. The secret burrows of the animals who had not fled were ripped open and their bodies were rent asunder, just like the soldiers on the plain, and body parts, human and animal alike, rained to the ground. Some of the animals lost tails while others lost limbs, and yet others were split in two by the

1473

blasts. The screeches of pain rising into the sky were not just human, they were animal as well. The lairs of snakes were blasted to pieces, scattering pieces of snake embryos left and right. The stench of blood mingled with the scent of flowers.

As the cannon fire tore into the men, blood spurted from wounds, staining even the clouds red. The first attack had targeted the centre of the crescent but didn't last long. Silence fell over the battlefield, and now it was time for the commanders to prove their mettle.

Blind Zeynel, Uzun Hasan's beloved son, led the right side of the crescent and he was poised to take on the forces of Prince Mustafa. Both of them, both Turkish, both Muslim, sat astride their horses swaying like cypress trees. Blind Zeynel turned toward the ten thousand soldiers behind him and gazed at the men in the front ranks. Slowly he approached them, looking each in the eye and giving them a silent blessing. In a voice that inspired courage, he explained the historical day that was unfolding before them:

"Brothers! The Ottomans are threatening the very existence of our country. These trees, this sky, the grass and creatures underfoot, your mothers, your sisters, and the fates of your unborn children all depend upon the swords you hold in your hands. I do not want you just to fight; I want you to stay alive. You may end up with only one eye like me, or leave an arm behind on this battlefield. But I want you to stay alive and save us forever from this enemy that has come to take our lands. This is our

1473

home. Creatures great and small are with us today, from the birds that spread their wings to the snakes underground, and some of them too will perish. You are fighting for your freedom, and they are fighting for Otlukbeli.

"Brothers, I was born with just one eye but I understand the world with two. Maybe I had to look at everything much longer than you to make up for what I lack. I've been to other countries and travelled other lands. And now listen to me not as Zeynel Beg the son of your sovereign, Uzun Hasan, but as Blind Zeynel, your brother, and have faith in me. The only place you will ever find your destiny is in your lands. I have seen the faces of people who found themselves in places other than their own, and their faces bore the expression of a longing for home. I do not want you just to fight; I want you to protect your country because then you will always have a home to come back to, no matter where you go. So may you be blessed in this holy battle. La ilahe illallah!"

When Blind Zeynel, who always wore a hedgehog quill around his neck for good luck, finished speaking, it seemed that the soldiers of the right side of the crescent had increased in height and girth, and even grown in number to the point that they outnumbered the Ottomans.

Meanwhile, Prince Mustafa gave his final orders to the Ottoman troops:

"Guardians of the Ottoman Empire, do you know why you are so far from your homes today? We are here to add to our empire the lands

1473

of the Akkoyunlu, a people who do not follow the commands of our prophet, who betray the unity of our religion and collaborate with heathens! We are bringing the justice of our sultan, Mehmed the Conqueror, and Ottoman might to Muslims who have been oppressed. But it is not just these lands that will recognize our empire; it is all the people under the reign of the Akkoyunlu. They will live according to the precepts of Islam and leave behind their shamanist ways, and the women will give birth to brave believing heroes like you. It was you who saved Istanbul from the Byzantines, and you will save Otlukbeli from the Akkoyunlu. Every drop of blood that drips from your sword will bring peace and prosperity to these lands. So fear not, Allah is by your side and his blessing is upon you. Every life you take will be a blessing for you in this cause, and it is your right. So go and claim your right, and be blessed in this holy battle. Ya Allah!"

As Prince Mustafa and Blind Zeynel approached each other, both armies shouting, "Allah Allah!" Mahmud Pasha, the leader of the Azap unit, was right beside Prince Mustafa. Mahmud Pasha was adept at handling the young men of the Azap, and he knew that if Blind Zeynel fell, his men would scatter too. And if Blind Zeynel fell, Uzun Hasan would fall as well. That's why he guided his men straight toward Blind Zeynel, half of whose soldiers had been wounded by cannon shot and gunfire. Some of the men's faces had been blown half off and others were still advancing even though they had been shot

1473

in the legs and feet. The handcrafted rifles of the Ottomans inflicted mortal wounds whenever they found their mark, and the advance of the Akkoyunlu was shaken and in disarray.

The Akkoyunlu had no weapons but the swords in their hands so they had to engage the Ottoman infantry in hand-to-hand combat as soon as they could. Otherwise, victory would never be theirs.

1473

"Ah"
       is the comma
              of a life.

1473

One of the tunnels my lover and I had dug opened directly onto the place where the two armies were clashing, and we rushed there. My lover wanted to see up close those humans slaughtering each other. When we poked our heads above ground, we saw thousands of scuffling intertwined feet and soldiers completely painted in blood, and when the sun shone through, their swords gleamed in the light. The crashing of swords and shields rang and echoed over the plain. It was the roar of war, nothing at all like the murmuring of a contented herd of animals.

Blind Zeynel galloped toward Prince Mustafa, who was himself fighting six soldiers at once. But when he saw Blind Zeynel approach, he escaped the melee and charged him. Both Prince Mustafa and Mahmud Pasha were bearing down on Blind Zeynel, their horse's hooves pounding the earth. Cries of "Allah, Allah!" shook the trees like gusts of wind, driving even the clouds apart. Then the two heirs to the Ottoman throne approached each other and stopped. Some of the soldiers were watching the events unfold. Prince Mustafa raised his sword over his head, Mahmud Pasha drew his sword with one hand and a dagger with the other, and then they both charged in for the attack. Blind in his right eye, Zeynel knew he had to make sure he kept both of his enemies to his left. In a few seconds they would clash, and either he would fall, or one of them would. Blind Zeynel muttered a prayer, knowing that he had to find a way out of this encircling attack.

1473

The horses galloped, frothing at the mouth, and Mahmud Pasha managed to get into Zeynel's blind spot. With a sudden thrust he plunged his sword into Zeynel's chest. Clutching the sword protruding from his chest, Blind Zeynel tumbled to the ground. Blood poured from his mouth and he gasped for breath. Prince Mustafa approached Blind Zeynel and leapt from his horse, glaring at his sworn enemy. Assuming that there was nothing to fear, he drew near and knelt down. Just as Prince Mustafa was about to draw his dagger, with his last breath Blind Zeynel grabbed the hedgehog quill around his neck and plunged it into the prince's eye. Hayyam had told us the story about that quill. Blind Zeynel had poisoned the tip of it and kept it for himself should he ever be wounded and captured by the enemy. Just then I wondered if perhaps that quill belonged to one of the two hedgehogs who had refused to leave Otlukbeli—it could be either mine, or my lover's.

Writhing in pain, Prince Mustafa wrenched the sword from Blind Zeynel's chest and cut off his head. The work that Mahmud Pasha had started was now done. He stood there in shock, as if that were the first time he had cut off someone's head. That shock must have made him forget the pain in his eye, which from now on would be blind. A few soldiers accompanied by a doctor approached and, helping Prince Mustafa onto his horse, led him towards a tent. At first the Akkoyunlu soldiers had been stunned by Blind Zeynel's death, but now they attacked again, driven by the rage of vengeance. Under Mahmud

1473

Pasha's orders, two Ottoman foot soldiers shoved Blind Zeynel's head onto the end of a flagstaff that they then drove into the ground for all the Akkoyunlu soldiers to see. The blood dripping from the head started turning the green Ottoman flag a crimson red.

Leading the remainder of the Akkoyunlu cavalry was Pir Muhhamed Alpavut, the right-hand man of Uzun Hasan. He had rushed to the right side of the crescent when he heard the crushing news. A commander who had made a name for himself for his courage, Pir Muhhamed Alpavut had also raised Blind Zeynel himself. He pulled down the flagstaff and removed Zeynel's head, which he placed in a cotton sack and, raising the sack into the air, he rode back the way he had come.

The sun was completely overhead and the trees had kept their shadows for themselves—sometimes they, too, are in need of shade. Uzun Hasan's most trusted commander, Pir Muhhamed Alpavut, was approaching on horseback. How is it that horses can gallop so quickly? And where do they run when not guided by a bridle? As each horseshoe struck the ground, dust rose up as these two bodies, horse and rider, bounded across the plain. They galloped as one, sending up clouds of dust, drawing ever nearer, two bodies like a poem with a single rhyme, a single rhythm. The roar of horseshoes shook the earth and long cracks appeared in the ground. Soon enough Pir Muhhamed Alpavut, still holding the sack aloft, drew near Uzun Hasan. A young soldier, standing in awe, muttered his name a few times, trembling all the while. The horse, whose black coat was as taut as a drawn bow and damp with sweat, slowed down. Free of any injuries, the horse lived on in a world of ruddy health.

Blood oozed from the sack. The blood was so thick that it took a long time for it to gather into droplets and fall to the earth. Such a wound could never heal; the blood didn't spurt but oozed ever so slowly. We were hiding behind some bushes, and my lover was shielding me with his own body. Uzun Hasan was standing just across the way, watching Pir Muhhamed Alpavut, gazing at the sack he held. He knew that the bloody sack was a bad omen. As Pir Muhhamed Alpavut approached, he reached up and pulled off the piece of cloth wound around his head, an ordinary piece of cloth, and threw it to the ground. Then he placed his hands on his head. This was a harbinger of what was to befall him. He ran his fingers across his face as if he wanted to tear away his very own skin. Pir Muhhamed Alpavut stopped his horse and, leaping to the ground, crouched at the feet of Uzun Hasan. His hand clutching the sack was still raised in the air.

As though snapping out of a deep dream, Uzun Hasan leaned over, took the sack, and then fell to his knees. A sultan would only fall to his knees because of love or the ravages of pain. He collapsed. When a sultan collapses, it is like a vast crevasse opening up in the earth, a crevasse that grows ever deeper as it widens. Uzun Hasan and the bloody sack were now in the depths of that crevasse.

1473

He opened the sack, reached in and removed the head—the severed head of his son, Blind Zeynel. His one eye that once had the power of sight had been laid low by the sword. That head was now completely blind. Blood had seeped from his eyes all the way down to his neck, which was a jumbled knot of veins and flesh. Only a human being could do something like that. No other living creature would ever think of committing such an act, but humans can, and they do. Uzun Hasan seemed to shrink ever and ever smaller until he reached the size of an ant. He gazed at the head of his beloved son, now utterly blind. What would he do now with that severed head? It would be his downfall, his destruction. Lost in thought, he gazed at the beautiful face of his son, which he himself had brought to that crevasse.

Blind Zeynel used to go for walks in Otlukbeli, and he never brought his horse. He would amble for hours on end, hoping he might come upon some of the animals of the plain and see them up close. That is why we knew his face so well. Once he had stretched out in the grass, letting the ants and scorpions crawl over him, lying so still that even the birds plucked up the courage to perch on his chest. I, too, had approached him, and I had smelled his arms and stomach. He smelled of flowers steeped in oils. It was a slightly cloying smell, but uplifting. If it had been anyone else, my lover never would have let me get so close to a human—but this was Blind Zeynel. With his blind eye, he was the only person to have captured the hearts of the animals of Otlukbeli. It

1473

was as if he wanted us to help him somehow, as if he thought that we could remedy the blindness of his eye. Animal after animal kissed that blind eye, but the result was always the same. Nothing changed.

1473

OTLUKBELI
STRICKEN BY THE AFFLICTION OF
REMORSE

Uzun Hasan, utterly alone in that apocalyptic crevasse, thought about how his son had been killed. He wondered if some soldier had snuck up on his blind side and lunged at him with a dagger or if he had been stabbed in the heat of battle. Of course, it was impossible to tell just by gazing at his son's head. When a father does not know where his son is hurting, he imagines that he hurts everywhere. And that is what Uzun Hasan imagined as well. He uttered not a word, wondering how he would be able to take that head back to his wife. That head, the only remaining part of their son's body that by now had probably been hacked into innumerable pieces. He crouched there like a boulder shot through with fissures. If the earth trembled ever so slightly, if the slightest of breezes blew, he would shatter into shards. He was weeping. When a sultan weeps, the rivers of the world withdraw their waters out of shame. At times like these, water begins to flow inwards, toward its own heart. A crackling ripped through Uzun Hasan's chest. His heart was rent like a horse cloven in two. He was withering away like a lamp that becomes nothing when it has run out of oil. When a sultan starts to moan in pain, animals freeze upon hearing that terrifying sound and they heave as if they would like to bury the sounds they make in the ground.

1473

With his groans, Uzun Hasan felt as if he was heaving up his organs. First his lungs would plunge into the crevasse, and then his stomach, followed by his intestines and lastly his heart. He wondered if he could create a new body for his son like that, or if in the end he should swallow them back down and begin life anew.

A shadow circled over all that was happening. Hayyam had come. This time he was there truly as a vulture to consume the remains of lives that had been taken. Uzun Hasan watched the shadow for a while. Then he looked up and saw the vulture, not knowing it was Hayyam, thinking whatever it is that humans think about vultures. He probably thought it was nothing more than an ominous bird that was impatient to devour his son's head.

For Hayyam, there was no difference between the son of a sultan and the son of a farmer. Death was the same for everyone. There was no need to search for any meanings beyond death itself. There was a crevasse and in the crevasse there were two hunks of flesh, one living and the other dead. That and nothing more. As Hayyam circled overhead, his mind filled with such thoughts, and he saw Blind Zeynel's soul, which was pure and bathed in light as it sped upwards into the sky. As they passed one another, they exchanged brief yet gentle smiles.

Once the soul has departed, all ties to the body are severed and the soul cares nothing for what becomes of the body. After circling for a while longer, Hayyam flew off in the direction of the battle and disappeared from sight.

1473

The crevasse had opened up in Uzun Hasan's very being, his masculinity, his back, his hands. He had become the crevasse itself. The pain was searing and violent, like a volcano bursting forth. How could a sword dare come down on a neck that was spryer than Blind Zeynel's foals, more elegant than his laurel trees? How could a human hand rend such a radiant-faced beautiful young man in two? For the first time it truly dawned on Uzun Hasan that he was in the midst of a battle. And that he should not be there.

The head of Blind Zeynel, the most beautiful son in the world, was left there in his father's hands like a solitary pomegranate in a desert. This pomegranate was bright red, and every single seed had its own story. And Uzun Hasan knew every single one of those stories. As those seeds began to speak to Uzun Hasan, waves of pain surged through him.

How had the pomegranate gotten here? How had it fallen so far from the tree? What wind could have blown it to the middle of that crevasse desert? Uzun Hasan pressed his son's head to his chest. But it was in vain. He couldn't take his son into himself. Mothers bury their sons in their hearts, but what about fathers?

With nothing left of him but a severed head, Zeynel was the same size as the day he was born. The place where Uzun Hasan needed to bury his son was none other than where he was standing, in the middle of that crevasse. He squeezed his eyes shut, and when he opened them, he tried to compose himself. He thought of Sultan Mehmed and the

1473

Ottomans. They slaughtered their own sons and brothers for the sake of the throne. Anyone without mercy for their own children would surely have none for the most beautiful child in the world. Suddenly he was filled with rage and a desire for revenge. But suffering still weighed heavy upon his heart.

He opened the sack and gently placed his son's head back inside. He noticed that his garments were ripped apart, and he wondered when that had happened. Slowly he was coming around, and as the blurriness cleared from his eyes, he could see the world around him again.

He now thought of his living sons. They were still out on the battleground, fighting the Ottoman troops. It was now time for Uzun Hasan to join the fray as well. For him, all of his soldiers were now Blind Zeynel. When they were killed, deep crevasses would open up in their father's heart for those sons, the most beautiful in the world. He knew that he had no choice but to go and finish the battle off at once. When he felt Pir Muhhamed Alpavut's hand on his shoulder, Uzun Hasan rose to his feet and handed the sack back to him. Pir Muhhamed Alpavut, who was known for being almost identical to Uzun Hasan in appearance, accepted this grave responsibility and entrusted it to one of his most trusted soldiers.

Uzun Hasan and Pir Muhhamed Alpavut were like brothers who had been born of the same mother but been separated and then reunited again. The soldier who took on the responsibility of safeguarding Blind Zeynel's head had but one task,

1473

and that was to protect it with his life until the battle was over. And he would stay alive to fulfil his duty. Uzun Hasan nodded for his horse to be brought over. He mounted his large sorrel horse and, with Pir Muhhamed Alpavut riding behind him, they galloped straight for Otlukbeli.

1473

THEY WERE NEITHER DEAD NOR ALIVE

The plain of Otlukbeli was ravaged and scarred with pits. That is why God never graces battlefields with his presence. For thousands of years he labours with wind and water to bring plants into being, and in one fell swoop they are killed. Stones are moved and the face of the Earth itself is completely changed. Could humans really rise up and challenge their god like that? Had they done so before?

It did not require a leap of imagination to guess that, each and every time, God drew his patience and strength to forgive humans from the natural world both above ground and above the heavens. He drew just as much from the mountains as from the stars, and from the roots of plants and the meteors that tumble from the sky.

At this point in the battle, Murat Cihangir, Uzun Hasan's nephew whom he loved just as much as his sons, was engaged in a fight to the death with Prince Bayezid on the left wing of the crescent.

Murat had a thick scar above his right eye. One day as a child he was playing at sword fighting with his uncle and he slipped, falling into a bush, and a branch jabbed through his eyebrow. Uzun Hasan, who already had a son who was blind in one eye, sacrificed thousands of sheep in gratitude that his beloved nephew had walked away from the fall with such a relatively light injury. He shared the meat from the sacrifices with the people, all of whom uttered prayers of thanks, and after those prayers, Murat lived a charmed life free of harm. That is, until the day of the great battle.

Murat had always been interested in literature and mysticism, and one of his favourite poets was Ali Şir Nevai. When he spoke, he would quote the words of the mystic poet Şeyhi, and he never let anyone say anything to slight Kaygusuz, who for him was the father of poetry. Murat longed to do what Kaygusuz had done and leave worldly matters behind, dedicating himself to nothingness. Who knows, if he had survived the battle perhaps he would have done that.

Some people carry songs within them, while others seem to effuse poetry. Murat Cihangir effused poetry. At times, the words of his favourite poets would flow from him, suffused throughout his entire being. As he was fighting, words flowed and he felt a flash of pain in his knee. An arrow fired by one of the Azap soldiers towards the left side of the crescent had found its mark, and he understood the spell was broken and the prayers had run out. Sometimes when people find themselves in great suffering, they think of songs, or perhaps of the poems they love. Murat thought of Kaygusuz's Epistle of the Body. When an egg took hold in the womb, the sun gave it spirit and the moon bequeathed to it a body. Every body part would have a corresponding zodiac sign. He thought of Capricorn, which had been dedicated to the knees of all living beings. The sign of Capricorn was

1473

bleeding. As Murat thought about Kaygusuz, he stopped thinking about his wound.

Prince Bayezid, who was commanding the Ottoman troops on that part of the battlefield, was known for his religious fervour. He performed his prayers meticulously, and thus garnered the respect of his fellow Muslims. But it had taken him much repentance to reach that point. His experience and the swelling number of troops he commanded quickly brought him victory.

Prince Bayezid was not just fighting; he was announcing the coming of his empire. When Murat Cihangir realized that he could not hold out for much longer, he made his way to the middle of the battle lines, clutching his wound, because he knew that his uncle Uzun Hasan, his cousin Uğurlu Mehmet, and Pir Muhammed Alpavut were there. Thinking that one day he may write about the battle, he carefully observed the battlefield, taking in every detail of that horrific scene. As the cannons and muskets fired volley after volley, Akkoyunlu soldiers fell, sometimes one by one, sometimes ten at once. That was how the left side of the crescent was being decimated.

Uzun Hasan never took his eyes from the sack holding the head of his son. He knew that it was impossible to win the battle. He had already lost more than half of his men, and he and his army were powerless in the face of Ottoman firepower. Maybe he was losing because he had underestimated his enemy, or maybe he had believed that his life had been blessed with prayers. In any case, he knew the

1473

battle would never end until he was killed, and yet he was driven on by the Akkoyunlu people's devotion and love for him. He stood in the middle of the crescent with Pir Muhammed Alpavut, and the two were almost indistinguishable. Neither Sultan Mehmed the Conqueror nor Uzun Hasan had yet brandished their swords or taken to the battlefield. As their soldiers were hacked down before them, they stood back, the guardians of their empires.

Uzun Hasan was standing in the middle of the crescent, which was like a castle that could not be taken, backed by the Akkoyunlu forces. Every cell in his body was howling in pain, and the sight of him suffering drove Pir Muhammed Alpavut into a rage. He wanted to charge into the enemies' ranks, hacking and slashing with his sword until not a single Ottoman soldier was left standing. The sky was clouding up, and Hayyam was flying in circles overhead. As the two crescents closed in on one another, getting smaller as soldiers fell, they joined at the ends, resembling an eye when seen from the sky. An eye that was bleeding in the centre, raw from being rubbed. Hayyam could not bring himself to take a closer look at that eye bleeding in the heart of Anatolia. The long, tenuous souls of dead soldiers flew up past him to the left and right as they ascended into the sky. Seeing them filled Hayyam with so much sadness that feathers began falling from his wings, one by one. Never had such suffering been seen in the world. While flight might once have been a joy, seeing those souls up close filled him with the most woeful sorrow of all. Anguished souls were rushing to the heart of God, and Hayyam circled and circled above, flying in ever tighter circles, overcome by it all. Who knows, perhaps he was searching for God. But some birds did not believe in God—they felt no need for such belief. No one could expect a creature that could look at the world through Hayyam's eyes to believe in God.

When the Akkoyunlu soldiers saw Uzun Hasan in such a state, they rushed in front of him, gathering in the hundreds and thousands. Their horses galloped faster than ever and the ground had never been flatter. At the same time, the Ottoman troops had gathered for their next charge. Otlukbeli was like a child that was ready to pull out its last baby teeth with its own hands. Soon nothing would be left but bare gums. First came the crashing of steel on steel as the two armies collided. Then wildly waving swords were plunged into bodies left and right. As the sound of clashing rang out, it seemed like it was not the soldiers fighting, just their swords. And they howled. The swords were raised up, and then they howled.

Otlukbeli was losing its teeth. Two sovereigns stood on two hills overlooking the plain that stretched between them. Neither Uzun Hasan nor Mehmed the Conqueror were making a move. Down below, soldiers were dying on the battlefield, covered in blood and flesh, and they stood there and watched. These two sultans—both of them Turkish, both of them Muslim—were taking lives just by standing there. Uzun Hasan thought often of the severed head of his son Blind Zeynel, and he pitied the fathers whose sons were being slaughtered one by one on the plain. He felt a sudden desire to say a prayer for their souls, a prayer that would never end. Pir Muhammed Alpavut had insisted that Uzun Hasan not join the fray, and he kept his word. He had to, for the good of the country. He was awaiting a signal from Pir Muhammed Alpavut. If Pir Muhammed Alpavut returned holding his sword in the air, Uzun Hasan was supposed to get away as quickly as he could. He had made that promise for the sake of his other sons and the Akkoyunlu people. Both armies continued shouting, "Allah! Allah!" If the bushes of Otlukbeli were to count the number of soldiers who fell beside them, they would have to count a soldier for each branch. They were fighting heroically and dying heroically. It seemed that if one gave up, they would all give up. The men who fell to the ground, which was covered in bloody mud, would never be able to wash away the stench. If the mothers of soldiers knew how easy it was for their sons to kill, they would never forgive them. Women whose children kill others first despise their own wombs.

Uzun Hasan was watching Pir Muhammed Alpavut. They had fought together against the Karamanoğlu, riding their horses in the eastern provinces and grieving through the same poems. Time and time again they had risked their lives to save the other. The same scholar had taught both of them and they both protected the Akkoyunlu lands for the same reason. But now, for the first time, Uzun Hasan was perched atop a hill like an incapable, useless coward while Pir Muhammed Alpavut was charging through the lines on his horses eager to kill, slaying Ottoman soldiers. Uzun knew they would never see each other or fight side by side again. Uzun Hasan had underestimated Mehmed the Conqueror, and he would pay the price for that by not being able to bury his son in one piece. He would have to tell his wife that they had lost their son, and already her cries of lament were ringing in his ears. Never before had he suffered such a defeat, and he was tormented by the thought that the Akkoyunlu people's faith in him would be shaken.

He wondered if he would be able to find some peace if he could give his life, if his soul were to be plucked from his body right there on the spot. A father who leads his son to such a gruesome death deserves the gravest punishment. He wanted what he deserved. And he deserved to die.

On the top of the hill, Mehmed the Conqueror thought about all the soldiers he had lost. Many more had died than he had expected. Now that the battle was in the sixth hour, he realized that he could still lose even though he had the advantage of superior numbers. What repentance would lead Allah to forgive a sin like that? What could ever justify Muslims slaughtering one another? Such a fate was so sinful that it could never be written in the stars. Such a battle could never be explained away, not in this world or in the next.

1473

Twenty years earlier when they had taken Istanbul from the Byzantines, he had filled the hearts of his soldiers with the passion of a holy war, and he had used that as a balm for his own conscience. It is not easy for a sovereign to create a country on lands that once belonged to someone else. When you conquer a place, can you then call it home? He had no choice. At the time, he was a young man, just twenty-one years old. But now he was forty, practically an old man nearing the end of his days.

The Akkoyunlu people would never embrace him as their sultan, nor would they ever send up prayers of gratitude for him. Above all, the type of Islam they practiced was quite different from his own. Life was hard for them, and they had to spend less time praying and more time working. Men and women could sit in the same room without thinking for a moment that it was a sin. They were well read and knowledgeable. It was not just the children of the court who were educated—even children of poor families were sent to the schools that Uzun Hasan had built. They did not need a religious scholar to issue a fatwa to know the difference between good and evil. Secretly, Mehmed was jealous of the way that the people were so close to each other and to their sovereign, and he was worried that, even if he won the battle, he would never be able to win their love and respect. If that were the case, why would Allah be on his side in Otlukbeli that day? Why would Allah want Mehmed the Conqueror to win the battle?

1473

I lodged
       my heart
              in your throat.

1473

It was early evening. My lover and I had witnessed so many deaths, and we could not bear to see one more. The Ottomans had lost nearly half their men, and almost all the Akkoyunlu army had been slaughtered. At long last, the day slowed down and darkness began to fall. A soldier approached us through the cloud of dust that still hung over the plain. He was in full sprint, holding his head with both hands, and his face bore an expression of such fear and horror that we were sure even his mother had never seen him so terrified. As he ran, he shouted, "Help! Help!" Then he suddenly stopped and he threw down the pointed hat he had been wearing and started stomping on it. Then he ran for a little more, and then threw down his shield and stomped on that too. We could tell from his clothes that he was a young Azap soldier. It seemed like he was trying to kill his shield. He knelt down and started punching the shield as if it were a human being. He was so close that we could hear his fingers cracking as he punched the shield, the bones in his hands breaking against the steel. Apparently satisfied with his efforts, he got up and started running again.

His cries were tormented, and they were horrifying to hear. My lover wept as he watched the man; he said we should do something to help. I took a step back, and looked at my lover, at his magnificent body. Flowers, green twigs, and colourful leaves were stuck to his quills here and there, sacrificing themselves for the beauty of his body... In their thoughts, they were showing how devoted they

1473

were to him. You may think that plants do not have minds, but they do think. As I looked at him, I felt a pang of jealousy.

Love was invented first, and it was followed by patience. Love emerged from every inevitable belief. I was in love with him. He gave shape to my world with his gaze, and whenever he reached out and did something, my mind would be drawn back in time to historical moments such as the discovery of fire and the invention of writing. Thinking gives love a form. I would think of him, even when he was by my side, as he is now. His arms were like marble pillars, indestructible, but at the same time, I suppose they could be destroyed. Maybe his arms were not so shapely but they were the purest white, and when he strode, it was as if he had just come back from travelling the continents of the world. My lover was a monument, from those arms that were the source of life to his quills, which were like a May morning. Humans and animals alike would line up just to catch a glimpse of him. But only I was able to reach into the depths of his heart, which was made up of the thousands of colours of the dappled moon. Such a journey never even came up in the holiest of texts. Everything was his doing: a bird suddenly taking flight and then perching somewhere, hills swelling from my body like the trembling of the Earth. Don't all waters, including Otlukbeli Lake, rise up to be one with the moon? He didn't bring me the flowers that I liked—he took me to them. As I was thinking all those things, I heard his voice:

- Run...
- My love...
- Go down all the passageways and get away from here. I will check on that young man.

Before now he had never approached a human, but God had made it his duty to save lives. I knew there was no way I could stop him. I raised my head up to the sky. Hayyam and the other vultures were circling over the dead, followed by crows. Soon they would be devouring the sons of mothers, the husbands of women, and siblings' older brothers. Nature was just doing its part. Piles of dead bodies here and there on the plain would soon be picked clean, giving life to new chicks.

Everyone was dying. Is time the only difference between a body and a carcass? Or is it the stench? The tombs built for some people are even grander than the lives they led when they were actually alive. The difference between the living and the dead is that one can escape while the other is prey that cannot flee. That and nothing more. So be it.

Do people bury their dead in graves so that animals do not eat them, or because they cannot open up a space in their hearts? Is it because they can only remember death when they go to those shrines? That animals do not have graves does not mean that they did not carry out acts of heroism when they were alive or that they were not loved, nor does it mean that they were wicked. After looking into my lover's eyes one last time, I did as he said and I ran. I ran... But as soon as I felt that he was convinced that I had gone, I ran straight back. He had already left our hiding spot and was approaching the soldier. Most animals have to take four steps for every two taken by a human.

The mad soldier had stopped and was panting for breath under a tree. My lover was drawing ever closer to him. It is suicide for a hedgehog to get so close to a normal human, much more so to one who has lost their mind. The soldier was weeping and moaning with his entire being, as if he was the only one to have suffered that day. Or perhaps he thought that the whole world was living out his particular destiny. He was utterly alone in the middle of Otlukbeli, and he kept repeating the same sentence:

"I killed my brother! I killed my brother!"

All of his friends were dead, he had taken many lives himself, and maybe he lost his mind when he shot an Akkoyunlu soldier who happened to look like his brother. Losing his grip on reality, he then started running, and his feet took him to that spot. My lover was quite close to him now. Unable to stay on his feet any longer, the soldier collapsed. He stretched out on the ground, clutching his dagger with one hand and a fistful of earth with the other. His teeth were chattering, and he was foaming at the mouth. Sweat seeped from his brow. I knew that my lover wanted to help the soldier but it was in vain. He turned his back to the man, pricking him in the leg with a quill but he did not respond; the pain in his heart numbed him to everything else.

1473

Even a few more jabs of quills failed to bring the moaning soldier around. Just as I thought that my lover would come back, he crawled closer to the man's hand, the one clutching the dagger. By watching the battle we had learned all about daggers, swords, and the tools of war. Especially daggers...

The man's face was purple, and he seemed to be waiting for death to take him. If he was left on his own there, he could wait years to die. It occurred to me that someone could take him to a doctor, and then he could go back to his village and marry the prettiest girl there, maybe even have children. My lover paid no heed to the dagger.

Minute by minute the soldier's condition was getting worse. When his trembling turned into convulsions, it was as if the moon had suddenly blazed in the middle of the day, Otlukbeli was cleft in two, releasing a gush of dark water, and everything stopped.

The world stopped turning,
rivers stopped,
blood stopped coursing through veins,
leaves stopped falling,
and yesterday stopped, today stopped,
the ageing of time stopped.
Frogs stopped croaking,
water stopped quivering,
stones stopped wearing down,
migrations, reproduction, and animals stopped.

When everything stopped, a hush fell over the world. I could not believe what my eyes were seeing. I looked again, and yet again, but my mind

1473

stubbornly refused to accept what I had seen. It did not matter that my lover took a step back or was frightened of the dagger. The shuddering soldier plunged his dagger into my lover's back.
Ah my lover...

All this happened because of the compassion my lover felt for the beating of hearts. The one and only thing he could not bear in the short lives we live was the stopping of a heart. Whenever an animal died in Otlukbeli, he went to its side, pressing his ear to its mouth to see if it was still breathing and pricking it with his quills in an attempt to stir it back to life. And he succeeded a few times, bringing a field mouse back to life and a peacock as well. But no power could ever bring my lover back now. If God had granted us hedgehogs a voice, I would have let out a scream capable of destroying Otlukbeli and raising it anew.

I ran to him. The soldier had fainted and my lover was in the clutches of death. His eyes, which normally flashed with fire, were fixed on a point in the sky.

> My lover perished,
> our children perished,
> all perished:
> hibernations,
> awakenings from winter sleeps,
> running by the waterside.
> His heart perished,
> as did his hands, face, nose,
> arms, legs,
> and quills.

1473

So that was death. Blood oozed from his back. Hunters had long sought the blood of hedgehogs, searching far and wide for it for centuries, believing it had the power to cure ailments.

Perhaps as the life drained from him he thought of me. Maybe in all this time the first time he thought of me was when that dagger was thrust into his back. Men think of women when there is no turning back, while women always think of their men. That is how he died.

My lover was almost drained of blood, and the divine being that he carried within him had burned out. His quills laid flat and his life in this world came to an end. He would never be mentioned in the annals of history, and no one would ever take heed of the fact that he had existed, nor would he be sent off to the next world with beautiful prayers or buried in a tomb. Vultures would devour him, and he would be gone, as if he had never lived.

With a grunt the soldier came around and rose to his feet. Looking around, he seemed to remember where he was and he ran back to the battlefield without once looking back at the life he had just taken, at the corpse of my lover.

For a moment I wondered if the vultures would eat me too if I played dead, but I knew they would sense the beating of my heart and leave me be. Then I thought of taking my own life by bashing my head against a stone. For the birds circling above, eating an animal was better than eating a human. It carried more honour. I knew that I had to flee soon

1473

to avoid seeing what would happen next. It was a struggle but I managed to pull the body of my lover into a knot of roots at the base of a tree. The longer it took the birds to find his corpse, the more time I would have with him in this world. I looked at his face one last time, taking in the divine light fading from his face, and then slipped into the nearest burrow entrance.

The world underground was like a womb, and I descended into it.

1473

A QUILL'S JAB AT THE FOUNT OF TEARS

The Akkoyunlu had long since lost the battle, and the largest chiefdom in Anatolia had been thrown into upheaval. When Pir Muhammed Alpavut realized the end was near, he turned his horse toward the hill where Uzun Hasan was waiting. Bravely he raised his sword, holding it aloft. He had been in the saddle for nearly eight hours and his body was stiff and sore. All the while he had been swinging his blood-stained sword, and his legs were trembling, his muscles on the verge of giving in to exhaustion. His eyelids were twitching and his legs uncontrollably jutted forward, and his spine was being crushed under the weight of his armour. His body was no longer his own.

The sword that Pir Muhammed Alpavut held over his head marked the end of the most ruthless battle of the fifteenth century. It was a sign that said meant, "Uzun Hasan, our sultan, it is now time for you to abandon the battlefield. Our sole desire is to be martyrs on this plain, so leave without looking back and remain as the leader of these lands." That sword was not raised to the heavens—rather, it seemed that it was being brought down on Uzun Hasan's neck.

As he had promised, Uzun Hasan grabbed hold of the reins and, giving his horse a sharp kick in the ribs, left the battlefield. He was leaving behind the place where his son had been killed, that plain where so many of his men had been hacked down by swords.

1473

As he raced away from the hill, he saw groups of people huddled behind boulders and bushes. They were from the local villages and they had come to see the outcome of the battle. Who knows how long they had been there. First he noticed women and village elders, and then he saw there were children as well. He knew that they had come to see how their fate would unfold. Uzun Hasan saw an army that had been defeated, but what did they see? As their leader fled, a leader for whom they prayed for every morning, they were wary of their futures.

He knew that when the battle drew to a close that evening, they would no longer be his subjects but those of Mehmed the Conqueror. Perhaps they would come to love him and embrace him as their leader, quickly forgetting Uzun Hasan. He wondered if they would read poems in their new leader's honour and toil tirelessly for him. Would they name their children after Mehmed and heap curses on his own name? As they watched the battle of Otlukbeli, peering from their hiding places, some of them witnessed the deaths of their children, husbands, and grandchildren. If he had not lost his beloved son Blind Zeynel in the battle, it would be harder to understand, but Uzun Hasan now knew that in their eyes he was both a murderer and a coward.

His horse raced onwards, still feeling the sting of that kick, carrying him away from those lands that he would never see again. He had firmly secured the sack containing the head of his son to the saddle. That journey with his son's severed head

1473

was the most challenging test of his life. If a sultan carries the head of his son, not a single animal in the world dares to move an inch. Bees will not draw nectar from flowers and birds will not take to the skies.

Uzun Hasan set forth, leaving his youth and past behind. Just as conquered lands one day become home, places that are lost become foreign lands.

Pir Muhammed Alpavut was relieved when he saw that Uzun Hasan had abandoned the hilltop, and he galloped over to the area of the battlefield where Mahmud Pasha was leading his men so that he could set his plan into motion. He was approached by some Ottoman soldiers and he let them take him captive. Looks of bewilderment spread among the Ottoman troops as this most prized of captives was taken. Pir Muhammed Alpavut proclaimed, "I am Uzun Hasan, the leader of the Akkoyunlu people. I am turning myself over to you. I request that you immediately inform your sovereign."

A commotion arose among the troops. Before turning him over to the sultan, they informed Mahmud Pasha about this turn of events. Pir Muhammed Alpavut's plan was working because no one in the Ottoman army had ever seen Uzun Hasan up close. Within a few minutes Mahmud Pasha appeared in front of Pir Muhammed Alpavut. Cautiously, he asked:

"Who are you?"

"I am Uzun Hasan, the sovereign of the Akkoyunlu people and the sultan of these lands."

"Why are you turning yourself over rather

1473

than fighting for your people?"

"So that my people may live."

"Are you Muslim?"

"Alhamdulillah."

"Tell your men to withdraw. These are now Ottoman lands."

Pir Muhammed Alpavut was taken into a tent and offered food and drink. The Ottomans hosted him in the way befitting a sultan, and not a hand was laid on his sword. For thirty minutes Pir Muhammed Alpavut waited, guarded by ten soldiers. He was covered from head to foot in dust, dirt, and blood, and he was exhausted.

It is commonly thought that people like Pir Muhammed Alpavut do not sleep or eat, or even have anything to do with worldly matters. You can recognize them immediately. They are resolute and make firm decisions, they are reliable and inspire confidence, and they sleep not to rest but to better understand the world around them—even in their dreams they remain dedicated to their causes. For the most part they do not marry or have children so that they won't inflict pain on others when they die, and hence they live solitary lives. Such people never engage in betrayal but they are always wary of being betrayed. History glosses over them, but they do not live for the sake of being recounted in epics.

Pir Muhammed Alpavut thought only of Uzun Hasan. Every second he was able to throw off the Ottomans gave Uzun Hasan more time to get away. He was composed, as if his entire life had been leading up to that moment. He knew exactly how he had to carry himself and he did not hesitate for a moment when he spoke. Everything was just as it should be. For Pir Muhammed Alpavut, war was not a topic worth dwelling on. When it was a matter of defending one's homeland, it did not matter if you killed one soldier or a thousand. It simply had to be done and you fulfilled your duty, nothing more or less. He was of the belief that animals existed for the sake of making life easier for people. As he sat there mulling over these things, someone entered the tent. It was Prince Bayezid, Mehmed the Conqueror's son. With a nod of his head Bazeyid commanded the person he thought was Uzun Hasan to rise to his feet. It seemed that he too had fallen for Pir Muhammed Alpavut's ruse.

"Are you Uzun Hasan?"

"Indeed."

"Why did you turn yourself over?"

"So that my people will not suffer any more than they have already."

"Your people did not give their lives for you. So why are you willing to give yours for them?"

"My people gave me something more precious than their lives: their freedom."

"They say that Uzun Hasan has a scar on his neck."

"That is the truth."

One of the soldiers quickly pulled off the piece of cloth wound around Pir Muhammed Alpavut's neck, baring his neck for the prince. The thick scar was convincing but the prince found it

1473

hard to believe that Uzun Hasan would so easily turn himself over. The face was the same, as was the scar. Pir Muhammed Alpavut had given himself that scar, right after the war with Jahan Shah in which Uzun Hasan was wounded. He had taken his dagger and sliced into his neck, and to make sure that it left a noticeable scar, he kept reopening the wound. He lost so much blood that he fell ill, and only when the physicians insisted did he let them apply a salve, and it took a long time to heal.

Prince Bayezid was still suspicious. The soldiers knew he had his doubts because the prince had not yet told his father about what had transpired. As he watched on, Mahmud Pasha glanced at Pir Muhammed Alpavut with knowing eyes; he had once been one of his men. Aside from being self-sacrificing, he was also a very compassionate man, and he did not say a word about the fact that the person who turned himself over to the Ottomans was not Uzun Hasan. He had only one thought on his mind, and that was the idea that a Muslim Turkish sultan might take a Muslim Turkish sovereign captive, and not just any sovereign but the leader of a powerful empire like the Akkoyunlu lands, and torture him. If they killed him, they would incite the wrath of the local people and maybe even cause uprisings to break out. Prince Bayezid called over one of his soldiers and said, "Bring me one of the Akkoyunlu prisoners."

The soldier dashed out of the tent. Pir Muhammed Alpavut realized the prince did not

1473

believe him and he was afraid that his ploy would be revealed. But it was not the kind of fear that makes your hands tremble or sends a chill down your spine. And he had already bought enough time for Uzun Hasan, who he guessed by now had gone beyond Erzincan and was making his way along the banks of the Euphrates river. In any case, night would soon fall and everyone would withdraw. Drunk with victory and the clean air of Otlukbeli, the Ottomans would fall into a wearied stupor. And if they were to try to pursue Uzun Hasan, they would not know in which direction he had gone. Even under the threat of death, Pir Muhammed Alpavut would not say a word about where his sovereign had gone, and no one else knew. So his ruse had worked, and his self-sacrifice and the wound he had inflicted on himself had not been in vain. Pir Muhammed Alpavut and the prince looked at one another. The expression Pir Muhammed Alpavut wore clearly said, "I am Uzun Hasan" but anger and doubt flashed in the prince's eyes.

The Akkoyunlu soldier who was summoned was in his early twenties. When he entered the tent, two Ottoman Janissaries grabbed him by the arms and another pressed a dagger to his throat. The soldier was trembling from head to foot. One of his sleeves was torn and blood oozed from a wound on his arm.

Life is measured not by its inherent value but by how much importance you place on it. For some, life is worth little more than a mote of dust, while for others it is worth the entire world. No one can be blamed for valuing their lives, and you cannot heap shame on someone for not giving up their life.

The young Akkoyunlu soldier clearly placed great value on his life. He was afraid, overcome by fear that at any moment his head would be cut from his neck. It was impossible to know what he hoped the future would bring but perhaps he was scared by the fact that he did not know what he might lose. Prince Bayezid approached the soldier and asked, "Who is this man?"

The soldier was no longer just trembling but shaking violently. He was unsure what he was supposed to say. Never in his life had he been put in such a situation; until then, he had always known how to respond to the questions put to him. Would he lose his life? Would his brave commander Pir Muhammed Alpavut be killed? Like everyone, he wanted to know what fate awaited him. The Janissaries gripped his arms tighter, and one jabbed his finger into the soldier's wound. This tribulation was the most painful of his life.

The prince asked again: "Who is this man?"

The young man looked into Pir Muhammed Alpavut's eyes but he was in so much pain that he could not make sense of what he saw there. Still, he was glad to see that Uzun Hasan had not been taken prisoner. He murmured, "Pir Muhammed Alpavut."

The doubt in Prince Bayezid's eyes flared into anger and he glared at Pir Muhammed Alpavut but it was in vain. His prisoner was clad in an unseen suit of armour born of fierce loyalty that protected

1473

him against all, even the fieriest of gazes. Killing him on the spot would do the Ottomans no good, and perhaps they thought he would eventually tell them where Uzun Hasan had gone if they kept him alive. The prince stormed out of the tent, followed by Mahmud Pasha. The darkness of night had fallen and fog was rolling in over the plain. They mounted their horses and rode up the hill where the sultan was watching over the battlefield.

The battle was over. The remaining Akkoyunlu soldiers had withdrawn and the Ottoman troops were walking among the fallen, separating the living from the dead. The plain of Otlukbeli was covered in thousands, tens of thousands, of corpses. Some hung over the branches of trees and others sprawled over bushes, arrows in their chests. Such a massacre had never been seen before in Otlukbeli. The sun set over the dead, shrouding them in darkness. Soon the plain would be buried in the blackness of night.

Prince Bayezid and Mahmud Pasha slowed down to take in the scene and they saw up close what their victory had cost them. The prince felt no remorse, as he believed they would bring prosperity and enlightenment to the Muslim Akkoyunlu people. Mahmud Pasha, however, knew the battle would be remembered for hundreds of years and that future generations of Akkoyunlu would carry that day in their memories. He thought that in the eyes of Allah, Muslims slaughtering other Muslims was an unforgivable sin. And perhaps he was right. After looking out over the scene they continued riding.

1473

Prince Bayezid and Mahmud Pasha approached the sultan. He was surrounded by soldiers and his face was illuminated by lamps that had been lit around him on the ground. The light flickered across his features, which reflected the pride he felt after emerging victorious from such a difficult battle. Never before had so much blood been spilled in so short a time. The soldiers were aware of that fact, and surviving such a calamitous battle was like a prayer in itself, a prayer marred by blood that would never be worthy of any holy book. Their faces were pale, and their glances were distracted. Beyond those proud visages lay the plain of Otlukbeli that had been cleft in two. Embarrassed by what he now had to say, Prince Bayezid clutched his dagger. Mustering his courage, he broke the silence and said, "My sultan, Uzun Hasan escaped."

A chilling silence fell over the top of the hill. At that moment, it was as if they were two complete strangers rather than father and son. It was clear the sultan was irritated by this turn of events and everyone wondered what he would decide to do next. Brushing aside all other thoughts, he turned and spoke to Mahmud Pasha as if his son was not even there: "Does anyone know where he went?"

"Yes, my sultan. Uzun Hasan's right-hand man and companion, Pir Muhammed Alpavut."

"And where is he?"

"He turned himself over to us."

Mehmed the Conqueror was just as surprised to hear this as the prince and Mahmud Pasha had been.

1473

"Did he betray Uzun Hasan?"

"No, my sultan. At first he claimed to be Uzun Hasan."

Matters were quickly becoming complicated. He asked, "Did you not realize that he was not Uzun Hasan?"

"Not at first. He has the same scar on his neck as Uzun Hasan."

"A thousand and one legends have been told in Anatolia about how he survived that wound."

"Indeed, my sultan. Pir Muhammed Alpavut inflicted that very same wound on himself after the battle."

Mehmed the Conqueror secretly admired Pir Muhammed's courage and heroism. He glanced at Mahmud Pasha and his son, Prince Bayezid, and he thought of his other sons, wondering if they would have the courage to do the same as Pir Muhammed. Who would dare to inflict such a deadly wound on themselves? Who would have the courage to turn themselves over to the enemy after such a bloody battle, claiming to be Mehmed the Conqueror? And to what end? To buy time so that his leader could get away and flee like a coward. But he knew that it was not the time to dwell on such matters, so he asked, "Did he say where Uzun Hasan went?"

They bowed their heads, their silence a testament to the fact that they had not been able to get a word from Pir Muhammed Alpavut about Uzun Hasan. Mehmed the Conqueror knew that Pir Muhammed, who was courageous enough to put his life on the line, would never say anything to betray

1473

his sultan. Yet again a wave of admiration rushed through him. He knew that if he had a commander who was so loyal, he would be able to take over not just Anatolia but the four corners of the world.

"Send a hundred men out to search for Uzun Hasan, each heading in a different direction."

Even though Mahmud Pasha knew every word uttered by the sultan was an order, he cut in: "My sultan..."

"What is it, Mahmud Pasha?"

"This victory is ours. Allah wants nothing more."

"What do you mean?"

"The Akkoyunlu are Turkish, just like the Ottomans. And they are Muslim, just as we are. Alhamdulillah."

When he said that, the soldiers surrounding them murmured, "Alhamdulillah." Mahmud Pasha went on to say, "It would be wrong for us to capture Uzun Hasan and take him as a prisoner or kill him."

"What are you saying? If we let the leader of our enemy get away, he will pull together a new army and lead an uprising."

"My sultan, Uzun Hasan is beloved not just by the Akkoyunlu but by all the people of Anatolia, even the Ottomans."

"So what if he is? Anyone who rises up against the Ottomans is a traitor. The people know that."

"Yes, they do, but if you have him killed, it will create unnecessary animosity."

"So what are you saying we do?"

"My lord, we should not go after Uzun

1473

Hasan. After suffering such a crushing defeat today, he will not dare rise up against us."

"How do you know that? Have you ever spoken with the man yourself?"

"No, my sultan."

"Then why are you taking his side?"

"I am doing nothing of the sort. I just do not think that making the Akkoyunlu any more of an enemy would be the honourable thing for us to do."

"We are bringing them the blessings, wealth and civilization of the Ottoman Empire. Why would they want to be our enemy?"

"The Akkoyunlu love Uzun Hasan as if he were their own child, father, and brother. If we take him captive or kill him, they will rise up against us."

Mehmed the Conqueror had little time to decide. When a sultan makes a decision, all the creatures of the world slow the beating of their hearts and the waters of the seas pull back. Mehmed the Conqueror knew that the death of Blind Zeynel would be a heavy blow for Uzun Hasan but he was not sure if that pain would be enough to stop him from gathering his forces again. And while he was not entirely convinced by Mahmud Pasha's words, he had to admit that they held some truth. At the same time, it made him suffer to see that his own beloved son, Prince Mustafa, had lost an eye. In the end, he was convinced that there was no need to anger the people of these lands he had just conquered for the Ottoman Empire, and he said, "Very well. We will not go after Uzun Hasan. But tell the men that we are

1473

going to camp here for three days and three nights. Pardon the captives and give gold to the locals."

Both Mahmud Pasha and Prince Bayezid were stunned by those words. Until that day, the sultan had never done such a thing after being victorious in battle. Messengers were sent to the troops on the plain of Otlukbeli to deliver the sultan's orders. Mehmed the Conqueror had tirelessly been preparing for that battle for months but that night, he would sleep peacefully at last. He withdrew to his tent and did not emerge again until late the next morning.

Otlukbeli began a new day, ravaged as it had never been before. All night long, wounded soldiers let out ear-splitting groans. Flies buzzed over the plain, feeding on the dead and wounded. The chirping of crickets merged with the croaking of frogs but they could not drown out the moans of the wounded. The sounds of the dying were unlike any sound ever heard, and they stirred feelings of shame in those men who had escaped the battle unscathed. Sleep, however, swept over even the darkness that night. Insects slept, reptiles slept, the wounded slept, the living slept, and the dead slept. After they all drifted off to sleep, Otlukbeli slowly exhaled after having held its breath since morning, breathing out long and deep. That breath tinged with the smell of pain, blood, fear, and life spread over the plain, and dawn broke.

1473

Love is the
        Kaaba of hedgehogs—
they circle
        around it again
and again.

1473

It seemed like I waited for months underground in my burrow. I slept, awoke, and slept again. Perhaps I aged. But the truth is I had only been there a few hours and my lover was dead somewhere up on the plain. I considered the possibility that he was not actually dead. Maybe it had all been a dream I had down in my burrow, a dream born of fear. I knew I had to find him.

It was the month of the parrot and the year of the tornado. Time had begun speaking in the language of nature. It became clear that the war was over as lives came to an end and the bodies of those young men were strewn on the ground, as the noses of dogs went dry, as the leaves that had fallen began to bud again. There was a hum in my ears interrupted only by occasional screams. It is said that the humming sound of battlefields can be heard centuries later. Even the winds, which had devoted themselves to God, were listening to that sound, and they too do not refrain from taking lives most of the time. The outermost ring of a tornado is the one that starts the storm but it is also the least destructive. In the end, we place the blame on the entirety of the storm.

All these loves, for nothing... We killed God for nothing. The moon was done with rising and setting, and dawn was breaking. Thick, rancid blood was seeping in through the entrance of the burrow. It had a sharp smell, as if it had waited a thousand years to emerge, and it suffused even the tips of my quills. It smelled worse than if all the animals of the

1473

world were to suffocate to death in a single cave. Otlukbeli was no longer beautiful. Not its forest, nor its lake. It had all died away: the ceremony of killing, the groans, the clashing of swords, the prayers, the pained cries... All that was left was the dampness of the blood that seeped into land. I went out through the middlemost passage, getting soaked in blood along the way. If my lover saw me like that, he may have thought I was gravely wounded, but it was not me that was bleeding, it was Otlukbeli.

The cloud of dust hanging over the plain was slowly dissipating. More and more birds arrived, fluttering their wings to drive it away. But even if we toiled for a thousand years we would not have been able to return Otlukbeli to its previous splendour. I stopped for a while, taking in the scene. The bodies of thousands of soldiers lay scattered on the ground like the shadows of the poplar trees that extended over Otlukbeli Lake, resting as if in imitation of those graceful trees. They had stretched out above their own shadows and died. Then there were the moans and the eyes locked on the blood oozing from open wounds. Everything had been laid low. Now, I was at the same height as those soldiers. I had never seen the faces of humans so close up, and there were thousands of them. I approached one, drawing ever closer. He was an Ottoman cavalryman, probably in his thirties, who had fallen together with his horse, magnificent animals that I had always believed were demigods. An arrow had pierced the soldier's neck and remained lodged there. Those projectiles of

1473

death bore no resemblance to my quills, and they were a far cry from all that is wise and virtuous. The first thing I noticed was the steel arrowhead. The blood trailing from his mouth to his cheek had coagulated and lost its red hue. His face had been crushed and most of his teeth were knocked out. He seemed to be looking up at the sky, his eyes focused on some distant point as if pleading for something. I wondered if he had seen Hayyam before he died. Bent at an impossible angle, his neck brought his head to rest on the ground in a final reunion. One of his legs was hidden from sight beneath the horse, and he was lying on his back, his hips twisted, as he waited to be devoured and reduced to nothing. That was best—to be eaten by the scavengers.

I was not afraid, nor was I saddened or brought to pity. They had not pitied each other, that much was obvious. The soldier had one hand on his heart and the other was still tightly clutching the reins, as if he might get up at any moment and continue to fight. If he pressed his hand to his heart hard enough, it would start beating again and God would give him a second chance. But he did not know that second chances are not given but taken. I started ambling about the dead plain, which was covered in bodies rather than stones. It was no longer Otlukbeli.

It was almost impossible to walk on the ground, as a fresh layer of death covered everything. I had no choice but to walk across the corpses littering the plain. Sometimes my feet would sink in and I would know that I had stepped into a gaping

1473

wound. It was like sinking into a marsh, and I had to use my quills and teeth to pull myself out. Each and every time I became covered in more putrid gore. I was now almost as dead as them. The leather sandals of some of the soldiers had fallen from their feet, and the tunics of others had been rent open, revealing the naked skin below, and their bodies were slowly being dried out under the heat of the sun. The tangle of arms and legs was like the knotty roots of a fig tree. Not a single body was rising up, and all was horizontal.

After a while I saw some of my lover's quills stuck in the sleeve of a soldier's tunic. I sniffed and bit them, as I desperately needed a clue that would lead me to my lover. The quill was still somewhat supple so I thought that he couldn't have gone far. I took one of the quills between my teeth and continued on my way, not knowing where I was going. No matter how hard I tried to pick up his scent all I could smell was sweat, blood, and gunpowder, but I knew that he had to be somewhere among those rotting corpses.

Some of the soldiers had fallen on top of each other when they died, and they appeared to be locked in an embrace. There were two young soldiers like that, one Ottoman and the other Akkoyunlu. The Akkoyunlu soldier was lying on his back, his arms wrapped around his enemy. They had probably been fighting and slain one another. The head of the Ottoman soldier was resting on his opponent's chest, and he seemed quite content. A snail was creeping over them, perhaps thinking they were nothing but stones. It would move forward once for every three times it paused. It is said that snails are born with a desire for death and that is why they are always underfoot when it rains.

This is mentioned in a hedgehog legend: When God created the world, he asked every living being what they wanted. Some asked for wings, others wanted intelligence, some asked for strong teeth, and others wanted to be able to fall in love. Still others asked for a shell like that of snails, as they thought that if they hid in their shells, they could avoid all danger, escape from the world when they wanted, and not suffer the pangs of love. God gave every creature exactly what they wanted and released them into the world, whereupon he also caused great storms to be unleashed across the face of the earth. All of the animals were injured, except for those who had wanted to be able to love. Some had cracked shells, others had broken teeth, and yet others lost their minds. Snails, which start life in the world already gravely wounded, always want to die and be reborn as a creature with the ability to love. So when it rains, as people and animals seek out shelter, they get underfoot in the hopes that their desire will be fulfilled, knowing that the armour of love is stronger than all else.

There was not a single being on the plain that could crush that unlucky snail, which by that point was crawling across the soldier's face, so that it could be reborn as something else. Death reigned supreme. The praying mantises, worms, ants, and birds slain by arrows, all were dead. In Otlukbeli, even death had met its demise. I continued making my way, still clutching my lover's quill between my teeth. The quills of hedgehogs point in every direction except for down. To the left, to the right, up, and every point in between. They live for eighteen years, not asking questions and hence not wasting time searching for answers, and they say that each life brims with its own knowledge and comes to an end in the same way, with no advice or precautions, always steeped in love. They gaze at each other in the name of the heart of the world. We two hedgehogs, born of quills in Otlukbeli, were plunged to the bottom of the marshes of history along with soldiers, women and children.

A little further ahead I noticed that a large tree seemed to be looking at me as if it might say something so I started walking in that direction. As I drew nearer, there still was not any movement so I started walking faster, drawn on by my instincts. What else are our instincts good for but driving us on, regardless of whether they are right or wrong? And so I was drawn ever closer to that tree. When I drew near, I saw that the tree had not summoned me for nothing. My lover's quills were scattered on the ground, and there was a bloodstain on the ground as large as me.

I sniffed the ground and picked up the scent of my lover. But if he was dead, where was his body? What kind of a thing was death? I had passed by thousands of corpses but for the first time death seemed real. I did not know what to do or where to go. I breathed in the scent of his quills; I think I was trying to understand what was happening. Neither my strong sense of smell nor the instincts that had brought me to that place were doing me any good. I was desperate and all alone in the world. I curled up, embracing myself, until I resembled a spiny ball. That was how all that pain shaped my body. I stayed curled up like that for a while and then I heard the flapping of wings. I wondered if it might be Hayyam. I uncurled myself, yet again taking on the shape of a hedgehog, and looked in the direction of the sound. Indeed it was our friend Hayyam, with his spotless beak and bulky body. He had left his eternal place in the sky and was coming down towards me. I waited for him to alight beside me, and he did.

    I had never seen him in such a state before. It is not often that you see a griffon vulture plunged into sadness. They are not overwhelmed by sorrow like other animals or people, and if they are wracked by anguish, they are masters of concealing it. Sadly he looked at me and said, "Your lover is dead."

    So it was not a dream. Everything I had seen was real and my lover had died at the hands of that mad soldier, his life taken by the trembling blade of that dagger. The reality of it all dawned on me at that moment. Howls of sorrow escaped my throat, much more loudly than you would expect from a body as small as mine. Even the tree gazed down upon me, lowering its branches out of pity. Hayyam had witnessed the death of my lover, and he warned the other vultures not to descend upon his body. Then where had his body been taken?

Hayyam had landed beside the body of my lover but, unable to bring himself to eat him, decided to take him to his nest. Piece by piece he carried him there, where he was fed to Hayyam's one chick, whose beautiful wings were not yet strong enough to carry it into the sky. I was comforted somewhat by the thought that my lover had not been rent to pieces by other animals. Also, he had not left this world but was living on through the body of that young vulture. I asked Hayyam where his nest was and he told me.

I knew that I would never be able to climb up to that craggy precipice so I decided that I would dig a burrow at the base and wait for death to take me. It would not take me long to die if I did not drink or eat anything, a week at most. But I had to make sure that I was not hunted down by another animal so I would have to dig the most hidden of burrows. Only Hayyam, that most beautiful of birds, would know where it was. For the first time in my life I asked something of Hayyam:

"When I die, I want you to tear my body to pieces and carry it up to your nest in your beak, and then feed what is left of me to your chick. That way, my lover and I will be reunited. By giving it life, we will be reborn in the same body."

Hayyam gravely agreed to my request, knowing he had to carry it out. He pressed his wings to the ground, preparing to take flight. I took one

1473

last look at Otlukbeli, which I knew I would never see again. It now looked so strange to me, as if I had never seen those trees, the limbs of which had been hacked down with swords. Down below, Otlukbeli Lake was stained red by blood, and it too was no longer the same. Just as they do everywhere, humans had changed Otlukbeli by ravaging it, as they always do. Taking a deep breath, I began to follow Hayyam, he soaring through the air as I crawled along in the direction of his nest.

I, too, was dying. Perhaps I was the only creature to die in that battle without losing a drop of blood. Nothing passed before my eyes. Death was neither cold nor frightening. Death was simply death, nothing more nor less.

1473

AND THEN HAYYAM...

I continued to watch Otlukbeli as my hedgehog's woes of love were inflamed by separation. Birds are of the sky, fish are of the water, and plants are of the earth. But what of humans? When do they truly die? Only humans taste death a few times in their lives, and only they live on for thousands of years, passed along in stories from language to language. I started taking to the sky, spinning around and around in the opposite direction of the earth. That is the only way it can be done. First the ground fell out from under me and then the air filled my wings. As I rose up, the wind dried the blood on my feathers.

All that remained below was getting smaller and smaller.

The people were getting smaller,

the dead were getting smaller,

the roses and cypresses were getting smaller,

the rippling rings on the water were getting smaller,

the lake itself was getting smaller,

the commotion, the tumult were getting smaller.

Otlukbeli was getting smaller and smaller.

As they shrank in size, everything started looking the same and the colours started to bleed into each other. At first, Otlukbeli had resembled a deep, red well. A red liquid with an oily sheen was flowing in one direction and then another. I could

1473

see where the bright green plants and dark brown soil had once been, along with the shores of the rippling lake. What was past stayed in the past. Souls flung from the bodies of people so mistreated in the world pushed and shoved each other as they rose up. What were they hoping to find in the sky?

Fires had been lit early around the tent of Mehmed the Conqueror. The sheep that had been taken all the way there just to die were roasting on spits. With each turn of the spits their flesh was searing. The gems on the sultan's green kaftan gleamed, showing where he stood. The sultan of the world was getting smaller and smaller.

It is thought that when humans learned how to control fire, they actually discovered themselves. But is that really true? Prince Bayezid was performing his prayers atop a large boulder; probably thanking his god for all that had transpired. So be it.

The prayers were getting smaller,

the worship was getting smaller.

Even with my sharp vision I was unable to see the quills, flesh and bones that were left of a hedgehog. They had vanished long before. Horses had lain down out of exhaustion, and they let mother earth scratch their backs as she shook. The pointed hats of the Azap troops were scattered across the plain. Some were moving, meaning that some of the soldiers had survived the battle. So be it. Mahmud Pasha was standing near the place where Pir Muhammed Alpavut was being held not far from the sultan's tent. These two men, both the right arms

1473

of sultans, were standing face to face, looking at each other, wondering which of them was braver, more devout, more deserving of victory.

Thoughts were getting smaller.

The women and children who had watched the battle from hilltops were getting smaller,

the elderly were getting smaller.

The villages and towns were getting smaller.

I was spinning, and the more I spun, the closer I got to the edge of the world. Otlukbeli was left there in the centre of the world. Uzun Hasan had turned and was riding in the direction of Mecca as he fled.

Uzun Hasan was getting smaller.

The sack containing the head of Blind Zeynel tied onto the horse's saddle was getting smaller.

Suffering was getting smaller.

Anatolia was getting smaller.

Then I could no longer see the traces of the battle or Otlukbeli.

The continents were divided by oceans.

Continents...

Oceans...

There were other red rivers in the world that were awash in blood. Wounds inflicted on dark skin flowed among green hair. Victories, losses, loves, loneliness, heroism and betrayals had all gathered into a single point and were indistinguishable. When the clouds moved in, all that happened yesterday and today was covered over by a vast expanse of white, as was all that would happen tomorrow. It did not matter what day it was, as the seasons were disappearing.

1473

      Mornings, evenings, joys, and sorrows were getting smaller.
      Time was getting smaller.
      I saw that my eyes were getting smaller,
      I was getting smaller.
      In a sky of darkness
      this world was getting smaller.
      Existence was getting smaller,
      nothingness was getting smaller.

Lightning Source UK Ltd.
Milton Keynes UK
UKOW01f1431200617
303763UK00001B/6/P